Things you can't do with Sausage Fingers

By Chris Sims

Dedications

Dedicated to my Fat-Fingered Friend Nick Pitt who goes through the daily struggle of having Sausage Fingers.

May your agony help others know that they are not alone! :)

Cooking a BBQ

Blowing up a balloon

BOWLING

Clapping

Using a Computer

Eating Pringles

FISHING

DIY

HOLDING HANDS

Lockpicking

petting an animal

picking your nose

Playing the Piano

Playing the Guitar

Putting your hands in your pockets

Sewing

Shaking Hands

SHOOTING A GUN

Taking a Selfie

Texting

Threading a Needle

Turning on a Lightswitch

Tying a Balloon

Tying your shoelaces

Using a Smartphone

Waving

Wearing a Ring

Wearing Gloves

Playing with a Yo-Yo

Thanks for reading.
If you enjoyed please leave a review and keep your eye out for more books on the way!

Chris